Double Dragons

by Enid Richemont and Ayesha Lopez

Chapter 1

Once there was a terrible fire-breathing dragon
who lived in a cave high above a town.
He would terrorise the townspeople, scorching
their spring flowers and tall summer corn
with his flames.

At night, the smoke from his nostrils would fill the sky and black out the stars.

One day, the dragon made a terrible demand.

"Send me your most beautiful maiden," he roared,

"or I'll burn down your town."

MOUNTAINS

TOWN

"I'll go!" cried Princess Greta.

"You're not the most beautiful," teased her brother."

"Girls can't fight dragons," added the king.

"This girl can," said Greta, and before anyone could stop her she ran outside, leapt on her horse and galloped away.

After many hours, she stopped to rest
beside a lake. Its clear surface shone
like a mirror. She could see her face clearly.
Greta stuck out her tongue, and her
reflection did, too.

"Hey!" thought Greta, "that gives me an idea."

Chapter 2

"Who are you?" roared the dragon when Greta arrived at his cave.

"You asked for a beautiful maiden," said Greta.

"You aren't beautiful. I wanted blue eyes, and long golden hair. Look, it's here in my book," puffed the dragon.

"Well your book is out of date," said Greta,

"unlike the other dragon's book."

The dragon spat out blasts of fire and smoke.

"What **other** dragon?" he bellowed.

"The one I met near the forest," said Greta.

"There are no other dragons!" said the dragon.

"Oh yes there are," said Greta. "And he was

looking for a beautiful maiden too – I should

have gone to his cave."

"Worse still, this place pongs!" Greta continued.

"And there are bones everywhere."

"Roast lamb may be nice," sighed the dragon,

"but barbecued knight is delicious!"

"Well, we'll see about that," said Greta,

and she began cleaning the cave.

Then Greta picked nuts and berries and brought fresh water from the spring.

"I'm not a vegetarian," roared the dragon.

"You are now," said Greta.

"Aren't you scared of me?" asked the dragon.

"Not as scared as I was of the other dragon," said Greta.

"I could eat you for my dinner," said the dragon.

Greta sighed. "To be eaten by the other dragon would have been an honour."

Chapter 3

At dawn, the dragon rose into the air and flew

off to search for the other dragon.

At noon, he came back.

"I saw no other dragon!" he thundered.

"I'll show you," she said and climbed on to his back.

"He's somewhere down there," she whispered when she spotted the lake.

"I'll get him!" roared the dragon. "I'll stuff his tail down his throat! I'll scorch holes in his wings!"

"Shh!" Greta whispered. "He's much bigger than you."

They landed, slithering through the bracken.

Then they crawled up to the lake.

"Look!" Greta cried. "There he is!"

The dragon stared at his reflection, his double.

"Aha - I've got you now!" he cried, shooting out

a tongue of orange flame. "Come out and fight!"

But the dragon in the lake just did the same.

"I'll scratch your eyes out!" roared the dragon.

He reared up and leapt ...

Chapter 4

SPLASH! The dragon's flames scorched the water.

The water bubbled and boiled.

The dragon's head rose up out of the water.

"You tricked me!" he roared at Greta, but he

couldn't swim and sank down into the water.

"My flames have gone out!" he wailed.

"Oh I'm so ashamed!" he cried, sinking again.

Then he rose for a third time.

"Help!" he spluttered. "Help!"

"I'll think about it," said Greta. "Will you stop stealing lambs and chickens?"

"I promise," glugged the dragon.

"And you'll stop eating knights?"

"I promise," gasped the dragon.

"But how can I trust you?" asked Greta.

"Dragon's honour," gasped the dragon. "Help!"

So Greta found a big stick, and pulled him out,

but it was too late. The dragon lay, not moving.

Greta pounded on his chest. She was sorry

she'd left him in the water so long.

"I don't want you to die," she cried.

"And I did like flying."

The dragon opened one eye. "But I've lost my flames," he wailed. "You should have let me drown." "Oh, don't say that," said Greta. "I'm sure we can find something useful for you to do."

Chapter 5

Greta rode back to the town, followed by the dragon, his head hung low in shame.

"She's tamed him!" cried the king.

"Hooray!" the people cried.

"Of course the beast must be killed,"
declared the king.

"Why?" demanded Greta. "He's stopped breathing
fire, and he's made a dragon's honour promise
to be good. In fact, he's become a vegetarian."

The dragon blushed. "Oh, the shame!"

he groaned.

"And I've just had another brilliant idea,"

said Greta, smiling.

A small airport was built in the town centre.

People bought tickets to fly to far away places.

It was the only way to travel! Greta and

the dragon made a great team, and became

great friends.

DRAGON AIR

Greta became the Royal Dragon Keeper.

She fed him and cleaned his cave every day.

And every night, after everyone had gone,

she and the dragon would go flying together

under the stars.

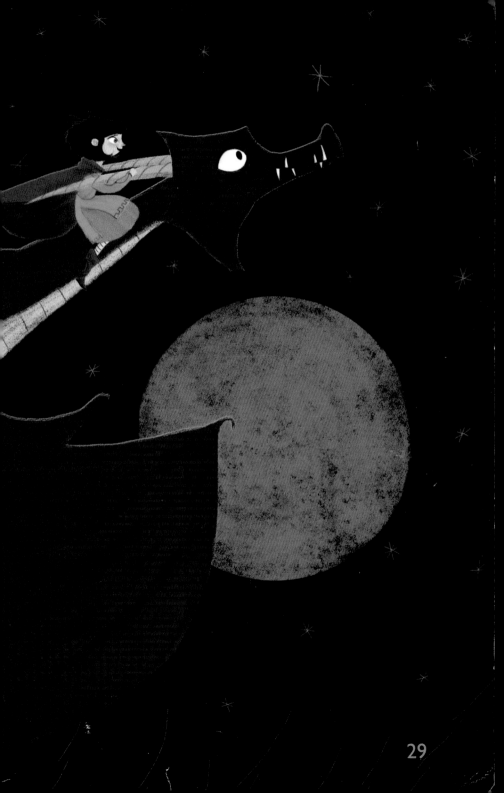

Things to think about

1. What words best decribe Greta's character?
2. How does Greta manage to trick the dragon?
3. Why does Greta then feel sorry for the Dragon?
4. How does Greta compare to other princesses you have come across in stories?
5. Can you think of any other stories in which a trick is used to beat a monster? Compare it with this story.

Write it yourself

One of the themes in this story is changing opinions. Now try to write your own story about a similar theme.

Plan your story before you begin to write it.
Start off with a story map:
• a beginning to introduce the characters and where your story is set (the setting);
• a problem which the main characters will need to fix in the story;
• an ending where the problems are resolved.

Get writing! Try to use interesting noun phrases such as "terrible fire-breathing dragon" to describe your story world and excite your reader.

Notes for parents and carers

Independent reading
This series is designed to provide an opportunity for your child to read independently, for pleasure and enjoyment. These notes are written for you to help your child make the most of this book.

About the book
Greta is no ordinary princess: she's brave, bold, courageous and cunning. She decides to save her town from a terrible fire-breathing dragon by challenging the dragon and outwitting him.

Before reading
Ask your child why they have selected this book. Look at the title and blurb together. What do they think it will be about? Do they think they will like it?

During reading
Encourage your child to read independently. If they get stuck on a word, remind them that they can sound it out in syllable chunks. They can also read on in the sentence and think about what would make sense.

After reading
Support comprehension and help your child think about the messages in the book that go beyond the story, using the questions on the page opposite.
Give your child a chance to respond to the story, asking:
Did you enjoy the story and why?
Who was your favourite character?
What was your favourite part?
What did you expect to happen at the end?

Franklin Watts
First published in Great Britain in 2018
by The Watts Publishing Group

Series Editors: Jackie Hamley and Melanie Palmer
Series Advisors: Dr Sue Bodman and Glen Franklin
Series Designer: Peter Scoulding

A CIP catalogue record for this book is
available from the British Library.

ISBN 978 1 4451 6301 7 (hbk)
ISBN 978 1 4451 6303 1 (pbk)
ISBN 978 1 4451 6302 4 (library ebook)

Printed in China

Franklin Watts
An imprint of
Hachette Children's Group
Part of The Watts Publishing Group
Carmelite House
50 Victoria Embankment
London EC4Y 0DZ

An Hachette UK Company
www.hachette.co.uk

www.franklinwatts.co.uk

For Phoebe Lane Stevens, with love – E.R.